·IN THE DAYS OF·

THE SALEM
WITCHCRAFT TRIALS

Marilynne K. Roach

HOUGHTON MIFFLIN COMPANY

BOSTON 1996

To the Danvers Light Alarm Company,
who helped save the farm

For information about this and other Houghton Mifflin Trade and reference books and multimedia products, visit The Bookstore at Houghton Mifflin on the World Wide Web at http://www.hmco.com/trade/.

Manufactured in the United States of America

Book design by Jessica Shatan
The text of this book is set in 13.25-point Minion.
The illustrations are pen-and-ink drawings.

VB   10   9   8   7   6   5   4   3   2   1

Library of Congress Cataloging-in-Publication Data
Roach, Marilynne K.
In the days of the Salem witchcraft trials / by Marilynne K. Roach.
p.   cm.
Includes bibliographic references and index.
ISBN 0-395-69704-2
1. Witchcraft—Massachusetts—Salem—Juvenile literature. 2. Trials (Witchcraft)—Massachusetts—Salem—Juvenile literature. 3. Salem (Mass.)—History—Colonial period, ca. 1600–1775—Juvenile literature. [1. Witchcraft—Massachusetts—Salem. 2. Trials (Witchcraft)—Massachusetts—Salem. 3. Salem (Mass.)—History—Colonial period, ca. 1600–1775] I. Title.
BF1576.R63 1996
133.4'3'097445—dc20   94-32383   CIP   AC

Acknowledgments
Objects on which illustrations are based are courtesy of many individuals and museums, including:
Danvers Archival Center: 21, 29, 40, 41, 53, 65 top; Essex Superior Court, Salem: 6, 16; Massachusetts Archives, Dorchester: 14; Massachusetts Historical Society, Boston: 67, 89 (0087); Massachusetts House of Representatives Chamber, State House, Boston: 60; Peabody Essex Museum, Salem: 39 (108889 and 101,850), 44 (E28561), 55 top (106,960), 56 (3182), 61 top (3188), 64 bottom (4134.39); Peabody Museum of Archaeology and Ethnology, Harvard University, Cambridge: 43 (24-7-10194279); State Archaeological Museum, Augusta, Maine: 45.

·Contents·

THE SALEM WITCHCRAFT TRIALS

In 1692, only three generations after British colonists settled the shores of New England, nineteen people were hanged for witchcraft in Salem, Massachusetts.

At that time Massachusetts was part of England's overseas empire. The witchcraft scare began in a rural corner of Salem then called Salem Village (now the separate town of Danvers). It spread to at least twenty-two other Massachusetts communities, and involved people from Maine to New York. But most of the trials were held in Salem.

In January 1692 the Salem Village minister, Samuel Parris, noticed that his nine-year-old daughter and twelve-year-old niece were acting strangely. They twitched, cried, made odd noises, and huddled in corners. Their family and the local doctors treated the girls for various illnesses but nothing helped. The cousins had frightened themselves with forbidden fortune-telling, but the adults would not learn about that until later. Weeks passed before anyone thought the girls might be suffering from witchcraft.

Late in February, at neighbor Mary Sibley's instruction, Parris's slaves (Tituba and John Indian) worked a spell to reveal who was the witch responsible. But the girls became worse and they began having seizures and visions. They reported seeing dim shapes they thought were the spirits of people causing their pains. When their family questioned them, suggesting names, the girls identified three local women. At this time two other girls, aged twelve and seventeen and living in two other families, also acted bewitched. Nearly sixty other people would follow over the next few months, mostly young single women in their late teens and early twenties.

The first three suspects—Sarah Good, Sarah Osborne, and Parris's slave Tituba—were arrested on February 29. When the magistrates (local officials) questioned them on March 1, Tituba told how witches had forced her to use magic to hurt the girls. But the girls' symptoms continued. A few weeks later a woman named Martha Corey was arrested, then Rebecca Nurse. Over 150 others would eventually be arrested.

Trials began in June after a new governor, Sir William Phips, arrived and set up a special court to handle the large number of cases. Lieutenant-Governor William Stoughton headed the court as chief justice with four other judges. Together they tried twenty-seven suspects in Salem at four different sittings and found all of them guilty. Another suspect, Giles Corey, refused to be tried and was pressed under heavy weights to force him to cooperate, but he died. (Pressing was legal under British law, but was never repeated in America.) Nineteen people were hanged at the edge of town during four days from June to September. Many more spent the hot, drought-stricken summer in crowded jails, where some died of fever.

Much of the testimony against the accused was "spectral evidence": reports by the "bewitched" victims of harm done to them by the spirits of witches that only the victims could see. From the start, most ministers warned against accepting this testimony. These spirits, they said, could be hallucinations or

devils in disguise. But the judges ignored this advice. Justice Nathaniel Saltonstall apparently disagreed with the other judges because he resigned after the first trial. Chief Justice Stoughton, however, was sure that evil spirits could not disguise themselves as anyone who was unwilling to cooperate. To complicate the trials even more, many suspects confessed when they were first questioned, frightened by the magistrates' accusations and the girls' convulsions. They also testified against the other suspects.

Two books by Boston ministers were published in October. In *Cases of Conscience,* Increase Mather explained why spectral evidence alone was not reasonable or fair. His son, Cotton Mather, agreed but reported in *Wonders of the Invisible World* that the court had listened to the testimony of eyewitnesses and defendants as well as to spectral evidence. By October so many people doubted the "witches'" guilt that some suspects were let go for a while on bail, and Governor Phips stopped all trials until English officials could settle the matter.

But some accused "witches" were still in jail, and many relatives were still asking for their kin's release. Phips allowed the trials to continue in Salem in January 1693, as long as the court did not accept spectral evidence. Only three were found guilty out of twenty-one tried, but they were scheduled to hang with five of the eight others who had been condemned the summer before. After some hesitation, Phips postponed all the executions and set the prisoners free (after they paid their jail bills).

By the summer of 1693, the English officials advised the Massachusetts court to use its own judgment, but by the time that instruction arrived, the trials were over. Massachusetts publicly admitted its terrible mistake in 1697. In 1711 the legislature passed a Reversal of Attainder, an act to clear the names of the condemned, although it forgot to list them all. (This was not corrected until 1957 and 1992.) Massachusetts also repaid the survivors and heirs for jail and court fees and for some of the property that had been taken from them.

As time passed and society changed, later generations found this whole era harder and harder to understand. How could people have hanged their neighbors for being witches? In the century after the trials, some people wondered what illness had caused symptoms that were mistaken for the effects of magic, but more thought the bewitched were liars or fools. Instead of trying to understand the tragedy, many people found it easier to feel superior to such a different culture from such a distant time—in the same way that people sometimes find other nations and cultures of their own century to be "strange."

The Salem witchcraft trials of 1692 were not unusual in the history of western witchcraft cases—except that fewer people died and the authorities admitted their mistakes—but they were unusual in the life of the communities involved. The fear of evil magic that led to the trials was common not only to European culture, but among the world's cultures. But the details of the Salem cases stemmed from the local life of New England at the end of the 1600s.

Unusual events happen in ordinary places among ordinary people. Yet what is ordinary in one century can seem odd to later generations. Customs or beliefs that are different from our own can seem wrong, but they are not wrong—they are only different. The Salem witchcraft cases cannot be understood without understanding the culture and the times they occurred in. This book is an introduction to the ordinary life of late seventeenth-century Massachusetts that surrounded, molded, and was interrupted by the Salem witchcraft trials.

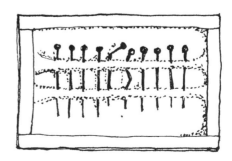

Witchcraft victims claimed the witches stuck them with these pins while the Salem trials of 1692 were in progress.

RELIGION

In the 1600s, religion was central to people's lives. Most people in colonial Massachusetts were Puritans, and Puritans suspected that the Devil especially resented their way of life. So some historians blamed Puritanism for encouraging witchcraft fears. Some historians also believed that the "witches" were accused because they held different religious views from their accusers. That was not true. In fact, most of the "witches" found the strength to endure the trials in the same religion as their neighbors'.

Originally, Puritans—or Nonconformists, as the British called them—were members of Britain's national church who tried to reform and "purify" the organization of their church. Most of the Puritans who settled Massachusetts called their churches

Congregational because each congregation ran itself rather than being managed by a board of bishops.

Not everyone who attended and supported these churches was a member, even when they shared the same religious beliefs. To become members, people had to undergo a spiritual experience they hoped meant that God would accept them into Heaven after they died. Toward the end of the 1600s, however, all a person needed to become a member was to be on good behavior. Members took part in the ceremonies of baptism and communion and—if they were men—could vote on church matters. They were also expected to behave better than nonmembers, so they might have their offenses criticized before the rest of the church or even lose their membership. (Rebecca Nurse, for example, lost her church membership after a government court found her guilty of working with the Devil.) As the Reverend Samuel Parris of Salem Village observed, a church was "a garden that has weeds as well as flowers."

Every Sunday, the congregations gathered in their meetinghouses. These plain one-room buildings were public property in most towns, except Boston, and housed town meetings during the week. Some of the witchcraft hearings were held in the Salem Village meetinghouse since it was large and available. Churches often called people to services with a drum, trumpet, or conch

shell. Wealthier meetinghouses had a bell in a central roof tower. Services, timed by an hourglass, lasted a few hours in the morning. After a midday dinner break, several more hours of services followed in the afternoon. Each service included prayers that were said while standing, Bible reading, a sermon, and psalms, which were sung by all and unaccompanied by musical instruments.

The sermon was the most important part of the service, so the pulpit was the focus of the meetinghouse. The minister spoke from it, to be better heard. He sometimes wore a dignified black robe over his clothes, but nothing fancier. The people sat on backless benches, in winter warming their feet on boxes of hot coals or under obedient dogs. Men sat on one side of the central aisle and women on the other, arranged by social rank. Military office and wealth counted for more than church membership, as far as seating went. Some were allowed to build themselves pews enclosed against drafts and stray dogs. Children, servants, and slaves stayed in the back or up in the gallery (balcony).

Communion table

About once a month, the long communion table was brought up so members could stay after services for communion. The symbolic bread and wine was served on silver if the members could afford it. Salem Village probably used pewter.

Pastors had to remind their congregations, as Samuel Parris reminded Salem Village, not to indulge "in unnecessary gazings to and fro, or useless whisperings, much less noddings and nappings." But many people discussed each sermon over dinner. Communities without a minister felt deprived.

A minister was expected to be well educated and to know the Bible and other ancient works in their original languages—Latin, Greek, and Hebrew. He was also expected to feel called by God to be a minister, and feel called to a specific church.

Ministers' salaries, like schoolmasters' pay, were paid by everyone's taxes, except in Boston where each church acted on its own. Householders were taxed according to their wealth. Often, instead of using money, they paid with goods or work—vegetables, meat, butter, cloth, a day's plowing, or even a swarm of bees.

By 1692, people of other religions lived in Massachusetts, especially in Boston. There were Presbyterians and Baptists, members of the Society of Friends (everyone else called them Quakers), Huguenots from France, and even Anglicans—members of the Church of England which the Puritans had come so far to avoid. These groups disagreed on certain thorny points, but all shared basic Christian ideas (and views of witchcraft).

Very few people were Roman Catholic, like Goody Glover (hanged for witchcraft by a non-Puritan court in 1688) and some French prisoners of war. There would be no Catholic priests living in Massachusetts for another hundred years. One or two Jewish merchants made occasional business trips to Boston from New York, but none lived any closer than Rhode Island.

Most of the people involved in the Salem witchcraft trials were Congregational, because most of the population was. Although some of the people accused were Quakers, like Abigail Soames, so were some of the accusers. Thomas Newton, an Anglican, was king's attorney during the trials, and the last execution before the Salem cases happened in 1688 when the government was mostly in Anglican hands. Beliefs about witchcraft and magic were not limited to any one religious group.

Salem Village's first two meetinghouses

LAW

Convicted witches were hanged in England well before New England was settled, and they continued to be hanged in England until 1736. Very few people were arrested in Massachusetts for witchcraft, however, compared to the ones who were arrested for theft and drunkenness.

Massachusetts' original code of laws was based on traditional British law, with a few biblical additions. Massachusetts law included, for example, the death penalty for worshiping idols (which never came to court), but made divorce legal and postponed the death penalty for robbery until the third offense. It was also easier in Massachusetts than in England for ordinary folk to sue their neighbors—which they often did—over broken contracts, unpaid bills, harmful false gossip, and the like.

The lion and the unicorn, symbols of Great Britain, from a decoration on Massachusetts Bay's 1629 charter

A county sheriff or town constable might be sent to arrest a suspect, but there was no police force. The local militias kept night watches in case of French and Indian raids or rowdiness caused by drunkards and other troublemakers. Private individuals or public officials could make a complaint against a suspected wrongdoer for theft, assault, or any other crime that threatened life, health, or property. With accuser and witnesses present, the local magistrate questioned the suspect. If this did not solve the problem, he sent the accused to the county's next scheduled court or, in cases involving the death penalty, to the higher court. Since witchcraft had a death penalty, it was tried only in a higher court. (It is the notes from the statements taken before the higher court met that have survived from the 1692 witchcraft cases, not dialogue from the trials themselves.)

Criminal suspects who were not considered dangerous might post bond (pay bail) to remain free until their trial began. The rest stayed in jail and paid room and board. Each county's court met for about a week, four times yearly. If that court agreed that there was enough evidence, several judges would then try the case and a jury of twelve would decide whether the suspect was innocent or guilty.

There were few lawyers in Massachusetts even after it was legal for them to accept fees, and they rarely represented clients in criminal cases until the early 1700s. Private individuals defended absent friends in civil cases. John Winthrop, one of the early governors of Massachusetts, had been a professional lawyer in England. In 1692 the king's attorney, the official who represented the government during the trials, was a trained lawyer.

Several judges listened to the evidence at the same time and were supposed to look after a defendant's rights. They were usually merchants and landowners rather than trained lawyers, but were well versed in local law. They took an active part in the trials, advising and questioning the accused, the witnesses, the jurors, and the king's attorney.

Defendants had a right to face their accusers and to know the exact charges against them. They could speak in their own defense and could also challenge which jurors were chosen.

A jury of twelve men listened to the trial, then met privately to reach a unanimous decision. Conviction required either a believable confession and evidence, or at least two believable witnesses of the same criminal act. (Witchcraft, like poisoning, left few physical clues, so courts gave more weight to indirect evidence in those cases.) A jury might find a defendant not guilty, guilty of a lesser crime, or guilty as charged. Judges could not overturn a verdict, but might ask the jury to reconsider it.

Although some of the "witches" in 1692 were accused of allegiance to the Devil, they were tried for supposedly trying to hurt people or property. In December 1692, a new law was passed in Massachusetts, reducing the penalty for witchcraft to a year's imprisonment for a first offense not involving a human death. But Britain objected to the legal details of the new law (although not to the idea of anti-witchcraft laws), and would not allow it. Instead of rewording the law, Massachusetts lawmakers ignored it and left witchcraft out of their laws. Although America's last witchcraft hanging was in 1692, England's was in 1713, and Scotland's was in 1722.

The seal of Essex County

PUNISHMENT

If a jury found a defendant guilty, the judges might order the culprit fined or whipped a certain number of "stripes"—the number could be lessened on appeal. (The old custom of whipping also was used in other colonies, even in Quaker Pennsylvania.) Or a person found guilty might have to stand in the marketplace wearing a sign stating the crime, or might have to wear a cloth letter—the first letter of the crime committed—for a longer time.

Judges ordered fathers to pay overdue child support, and ordered thieves to pay three times the amount they had stolen, even if they had to be sold as bond servants to do it. (A bond servant had to work a fixed number of years before being freed.) People who stole more than once might be branded on the

17

forehead. Those guilty of slander might have an ear clipped if their remarks were aimed at the government. For insulting private citizens, they might wear a cleft stick on their tongues for a few hours in public. Acting sorry helped, but some offenders had to promise they would pay a fine if they did not behave, prove they could pay it, and report to the next scheduled court. Those found guilty could appeal.

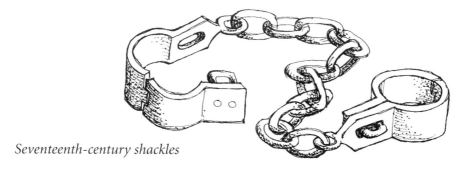

Seventeenth-century shackles

Few people were sentenced to prison. Imprisonment was not a usual punishment in those days. Prison was where people waited to be tried. The Essex County jails in Salem and Ipswich were built of wood but were more sturdy than ordinary houses. Boston's jail was built of stone. Wealthy suspects like Philip English might rent a better room in the prison-keeper's home.

Some prisoners were shackled, and had to pay for their iron bonds along with room and board. A few burrowed under walls or removed windows bars to escape. Others died in jail of disease, especially while prisons were overcrowded during the witchcraft year. Jails were always dirty. One of the Boston prison's expenses in 1690 was five shillings to the man who removed "several loads of dung out of the cellar."

Those sentenced to death—pirates, murderers, witches—were hanged in public as a warning to others who might break the law. All earlier Massachusetts executions had taken place in Boston. So had the trials that had preceded them. Since the "witches" were tried in Salem in 1692, the hangings took place there, on a rocky pasture at the edge of town. People assumed that everyone faced a heavenly judgment after death, so the condemned were allowed to have the minister of their choice pray with them before being hanged.

At the gallows, the convicted would stand, one at a time, partway up a ladder. Blindfolded, with their hands tied behind them, they would then be pushed off. Death was not always quick. This was the fate that faced the people condemned of witchcraft.

WITCHES

What people in seventeenth-century New England believed about witches was much older than their own English culture. Ancient Romans, for example, condemned sorcerers to be burned, and Roman literature described evil witches as well as kindly goddesses.

Some people wondered if magic might be a natural ability. But most of the colonists, like most people in Europe, thought magic was unnatural for people; it was something only spirits could do. Only evil spirits—devils—would work evil magic, and Satan was the devils' leader. Witches, folk concluded, worked with Satan. If witches thought they made their own magic, that was because the devils fooled them into believing it.

Witches, tradition said, envied their neighbors' luck, and would spoil their crops or even kill to get back at them. Witches gave their souls to Hell for the power of working hurtful magic. They could work spells invisibly or at a distance. Or a witch could send a "familiar spirit" (a cooperating devil) in animal form to do the job. A victim might think he saw witches making magic, then see them disappear. Frightened people forgot they also believed that devils could assume *anyone's* form as a disguise to spread false suspicion. In 1692 the court acted as if devils could impersonate only witches.

Anyone might be a witch, but most New England suspects were (as in many other cultures) poor older widows. Only one in four suspects was a man, and fewer men were brought to trial. When men bragged of magical powers, then denied it in court, their denials were believed. Accused women rarely made such boasts, and when they denied they were witches, they were less often believed.

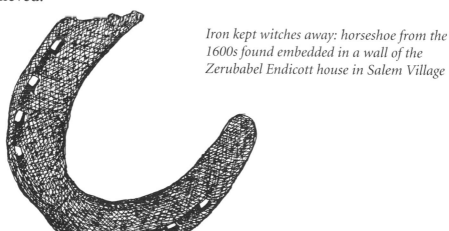

Iron kept witches away: horseshoe from the 1600s found embedded in a wall of the Zerubabel Endicott house in Salem Village

In 1692 many suspects confessed to witchcraft from fear. The records show that most suspects did not consider themselves to be witches. At least a year before the Salem scare, Abigail Hobbs told her Topsfield neighbors that she had sold herself to the Devil, but most of them thought she was just rude and reckless. Fourteen-year-old Abraham Ireland of Charlestown wrote a contract for his soul in 1685. The court ordered him to be whipped, not for being a witch, but for making such a dangerous invitation to evil spirits.

A suspected witch's accusers were usually neighbors whose families and livelihood seemed threatened—men whose farm animals died for no known reason, women whose children myste-riously sickened. But suspicions remained private unless other neighbors agreed that a suspect could be a witch. Even then, fears might not spread if community leaders discouraged them. And if a case did reach the county court, it might be dismissed. Usually, ministers advised the supposed victims to think about how their own actions might have caused their difficulties. Magistrates warned against the destructive power of gossip. But in 1692, authorities were faced with dozens of bewitched victims who were having violent seizures and other physical problems.

Most of these were teenage girls. A few were younger girls,

some were married women, and others were men. Later genera-tions thought their symptoms had been the result of an unknown physical illness, of overexcitement in the "weaker" female brain (the bewitched men having been forgotten), of a fungus that had poisoned their rye bread, of unhappy childhoods, or of lies and no real illness at all.

The convulsions, which were rare in witchcraft cases, do resemble the symptoms that result from certain physical and mental states that are caused by fear. When a frightened person breathes very quickly, it can upset the oxygen flow to the brain and cause convulsions. A few bewitched accusers had faked their illnesses, but most of them appear to have had real symptoms that stemmed from an unknown and tragically misunderstood cause. At least six of the bewitched died.

Sacke & Sugar

Jarmara

Vinegar Tom

Newes

Holt

English witches' familiars and their names

Between 1638 and 1691, more than 120 people throughout New England were suspected of witchcraft. They made up 90 percent of British America's recorded witch suspects. Some were in court over and over, while others never came to trial. A third of those who did appear in court were there to sue their neighbors for calling them witches—and they often won. Of the other two-thirds of witchcraft cases, about twenty-two ended in guilty verdicts. Surviving court records are incomplete but show that sixteen people were hanged, and six people (five women and one man) had their verdicts reversed or ignored.

In Europe, suspects had been condemned and executed by the thousands during the 1400s and 1500s. Fewer died in England, but around 1645 more were hanged in one county than were ever hanged in all of New England. Although British and European witchcraft trials were no longer as common by the end of the 1600s, New Englanders were well aware of cases overseas.

Salem's trials, however, would be better remembered than all the rest, as if no other culture had ever tried to fight against the work of evil spirits and their human helpers.

Salem witches' familiars

THE INVISIBLE WORLD

Magic, according to folk tradition, affected the ordinary world but began in the invisible world of spirits— good, evil, and neutral. People's immortal souls were expected to leave for Heaven or Hell after their bodies died and were not supposed to stay in this world as ghosts. But ghosts were reported in New England all the same. (According to the bewitched, several ghosts came to the trials in 1692 and accused the "witches" of murder by magic.) The idea of nature spirits, like elves, was fading from British culture in England and the colonies, yet at least one Salem woman set out clean water each night for the fairies.

But the more widely accepted biblical view was that the only spirits other than God and human beings were angels. These

beings (the good angels faithful to God and the rebellious ones who became devils) swarmed in greater numbers than summer mosquitoes, far outnumbering people.

By tradition, most angels were good, delighting in helping and being helped by people. Invisible and unsuspected, they encouraged folk to do good deeds. The people who did report seeing them described everything from majestic winged beings to motherly figures mistaken for neighbors. In 1692, the bewitched spoke of a shining man who drove away the evil spirits, but some people doubted that tale.

Devils, according to the testimony of the bewitched and the "confessed" witches, appeared as men, dogs, hogs, flies, and angels of light. As everyone knew, devils might work with a witch or make trouble on their own as they disturbed a victim's mind or body, worsening existing illnesses or creating new ones. Evil imps whispered temptation at home, in the meetinghouse, and at the marketplace. Some wicked people were deliberately loyal to the Devil in return for the power of evil magic: that was what it meant to be a witch as the law then defined it. Even so, people assumed that most misfortune had only earthly causes.

The greatest influence of all, however, was God, who frequently

worked through nature. Even storms or illness could be a warning to the careless, a punishment to the guilty, or a test for the good. A bountiful harvest, a rescue at sea, or a recovery from sickness could also be the work of God.

The reality of a spirit world was accepted by all cultures in the late 1600s, from the native Algonquin of New England to the French court, which had its own witchcraft scandal in 1680. Even the seventeenth-century founders of modern science, like the chemist Robert Boyle and the physicist Sir Isaac Newton, were as interested in the invisible world as in the visible physical world whose natural laws they discovered.

Unusual events might be messages from the invisible world. Sailors reported a helpful figure called White Hat who patrolled Newfoundland's coast and warned sailors before storms. In Massachusetts, watchers in Lynn were puzzled when they saw clouds form a sailing ship and an armed giant over the sea. A man reported talking with an angel under a tree in Braintree, but his neighbors didn't believe him. Although none of these sightings was explained, they seemed no more unlikely than tales of mermaids. The world was full of unexplained wonders and the possibility of magic was a part of everyday life.

MAGIC

If magic could harm, some people thought, then it might also help. But ministers thought that the idea of neutral or good magic was both illogical and a dangerous invitation to devils. Yet even the most respectful congregation did not always agree with its pastor, or suppose that a college education taught a man everything. Mary Sibley suggested a charm to reveal who had bewitched the Reverend Parris's girls in 1692, even though she was a member of the Salem Village church.

Magic seemed to work often enough that many believed it was real or at least worth a try. A clear understanding of magic seemed unnecessary. Bakers, after all, did not need to understand why yeast made wheat bread rise in order to cook a loaf. Many thought that magical results, like fortune telling, were the work of holy angels, a gift from God, or a natural scientific reaction. Modern scientific study was just beginning and still included much that would later be thought magical, like trying to turn lead into gold. Ministers warned against inviting what could only be the work of evil spirits. But the cause of apparently magical effects was not always clear.

Many people tried homemade charms or consulted local experts whom the English called cunning folk, blessing witches, or good witches. In New England these names seemed too close to "witch" for the experts to use them. Some cunning folk sold charms—prayers written on papers sealed with wax, for example—to prevent illness. Others cured toothaches, fevers, warts, or wounds by saying a rhyme over them. The folk healer Roger Toothaker (who was accused of witchcraft in 1692) hunted

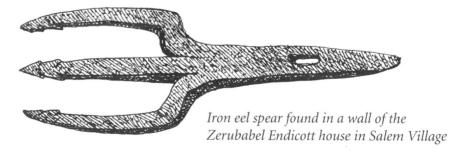

Iron eel spear found in a wall of the Zerubabel Endicott house in Salem Village

witches and even claimed to have killed one with a counterspell.

Such "little sorceries" were everywhere in New England. Respectable booksellers carried volumes of political predictions based on astronomy. People owned books that taught palm

reading and astrology, and anyone could tell fortunes with common household objects. They balanced a sieve between two scissor blades, or tied a Bible around a large key clamped between its pages like a bookmark (which bowed its covers). Two people would balance either of these unsteady arrangements between them, and would let slight twitches answer their questions about lost items or missing kin. In the patterns made by nails dropped in grease, or the forms an egg white took in water, girls tried to find out who would be their sweethearts.

People tried to keep evil magic from a house by surrounding it with sprigs of laurel or nailing an iron horseshoe over its front door. They hung a hole-stone (a stone with a hole that had formed naturally) in the stable to keep evil spirits away from livestock. Judge Sewall's cousin recommended that he wrap something scarlet (the color of life) around his sick child's head. Much of this seemed natural rather than magical.

If something evil happened, people might try to turn the bad luck back on the witch. As Toothaker had, they might boil, burn, or damage a piece of the bewitched victim because they believed it was magically attached to the evildoer. The witch, then, would feel whatever was done to the hair. More desperate people might thrust red-hot pokers in churns that wouldn't make butter (to burn the guilty witch), or scratch a "witch" to let the flowing blood wash away the magic.

Magical folk customs were so common that even the Salem court accepted them in the confusions of 1692. Magistrates listened as people accusing neighbors of witchcraft described their own tries at countermagic. The magistrates ordered the touch test, believing it was scientific, to end the bewitched girls' seizures. They thought that evil powers traveled outward with a witch's eyesight, and that when a witch touched a victim this would draw out the eye poison. The bewitched expected relief from this test, so they sometimes relaxed when they were touched. Reverend Increase Mather, aware of Newton's discoveries about sight, disagreed. Gossiping tongues, Mather said, did more harm than evil eyes, which he did not believe in.

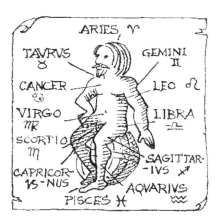

THE LAND

The area that would become the United States was still mostly unknown to the European newcomers. English colonies stretched from Maine (part of which was claimed by France) to Carolina (part of which was claimed by Spain). In the west, California belonged to Mexico, and European settlement had not yet begun there. The native peoples of the central prairies had seen the horses that had escaped from the strangers' few settlements, but had not yet tamed them.

New England's own settlements clustered mainly near the sea and up the rivers, with fewer to the north and east near French territory. Wilderness was never far away, but by the century's end, walrus seldom visited Massachusetts Bay, and old-timers thought the vast flocks of passenger pigeons were smaller than they had been in their youth. (The birds would become extinct in 1914.) The land itself was changing. Erosion had washed some houses into Salem harbor after the trees on Winter Island were cut down and no longer blocked the force of storms. But the great salt marshes still stretched along the coast, and wooded swamps filled the hollows among pastures and orchards. Wolves and bears still prowled the edges of towns.

In the 1630s, some of the earliest English settlers had shivered through their first winter in dugouts. Three generations later, Boston, the "Metropolis of New England" and capital of the Province of Massachusetts Bay, was the largest city in British North America, with more than 5,000 inhabitants. (The French called all New Englanders "Bostonaise.")

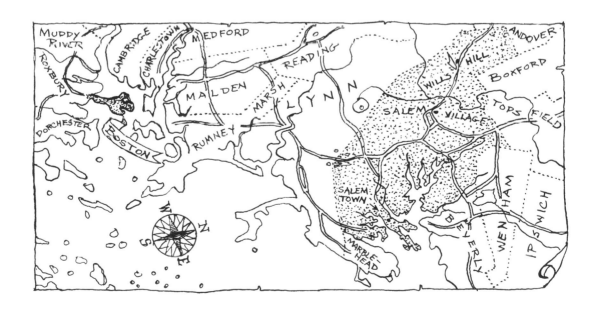

Judge Jonathan Corwin's house in Salem

Salem, a half day's journey north by horseback or boat, was older but smaller, with a population one quarter the size of Boston's. Most of the homes there clustered on a neck of land between two rivers. Besides the wooden, town-owned meeting-house, Salem had a small brick Town House. The Latin Grammar School used the ground floor, and town meetings or the occasional county court met upstairs.

Inland, the main road ran toward the steep public pasture that would one day be called Gallows Hill after nineteen people were hanged there for witchcraft. The area of farms called Salem Village lay northwest of the harbor. About 550 people or fewer lived there in about 90 households linked by a few dirt roads.

All streets were dirt, except for those in the center of Boston, and were shared by walkers, wagons, horses, and cattle. In Salem Village, a small building for the militiamen keeping watch, a tavern, the meetinghouse, and a few craftsmen's shops stood near the crossroads. But most people lived at a distance, their farm-houses set off among the fields and wood lots, a long walk from town.

WORLDLY GOODS

T he everyday life of the people in this New England landscape reflected English customs adapted to the local climate and available supplies.

Seventeenth-century New Englanders dressed in layers of linen and wool to protect themselves against the weather—much colder in winter and hotter in summer than England's. Laborers sometimes worked in ankle-length protective pants, but most men wore knee-length breeches. Warm stockings were so necessary that even the bewitched girls continued to knit between seizures. A man usually wore a linen shirt under a knee-length waistcoat (vest) and a full-skirted coat. Most tied on neckcloths instead of wearing the old-fashioned starched linen collars, although ministers still wore a version of them.

A woman wore a bodice over her linen shift, along with several layers of skirts (always called petticoats or coats). Most wardrobes were limited enough that people (or their spirits) could be identified by their clothes, like Bridget Bishop with her red bodice. Some men and women bought imported goods, even silk, of a dignified black or cheerful scarlet, but these colors were expensive. Less expensive cloth was dyed in more muted earthy tones.

Grown women pinned up their long hair under a linen cap or hood for modesty and neatness. Men wore broad-brimmed hats. Their shoulder-length hair was longer than their grandfathers had thought decent. Some city men even wore periwigs, cutting off their own hair and putting on big, expensive bushes of someone else's.

Most people's homes, in town or country, were built in the style brought from the Midlands and southeast England: one room, with perhaps another one above it, then garret space or a loft above that under a sloping roof, and a huge chimney stack filling one end wall. Larger houses, like the Salem Village parsonage, had two or more rooms per floor, one on each side of the chimney to save its warmth. But the great hearth drew much of the fire's heat straight up the flue, and the cost of fuel was a constant worry.

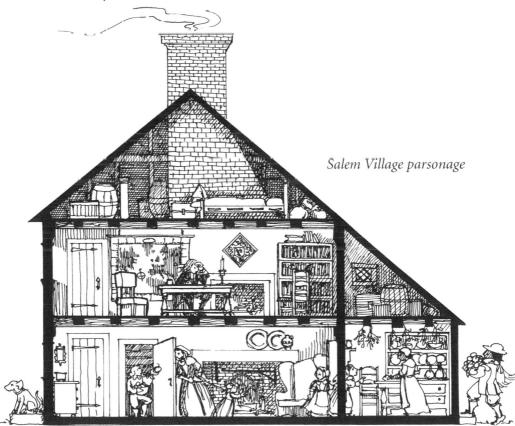

Salem Village parsonage

Houses from the 1600s

Almost all houses were made of wood, covered with wooden shingles or long clapboards to protect against the weather, although some newer houses in Boston were brick. Most homes were crowded with children, apprentices, relatives, and servants either free or enslaved. Even in simple homes a housewife needed more than one pair of hands to keep a family fed and cared for. Lean-tos, additions, and attached workshops provided more space for the farmwork, food preparation and storage, and small crafts (like weaving or shoemaking) that were done in a family's living space. Some homeowners walled off the corner of one room and rented the space to a boarder.

A family's indoor life centered on the hall—the main room— and its hearth, which was the household's main source of heat and light. Some people had a few chairs and a table, but most sat on stools and benches, or on the chests in which they stored their clothes and linens (sheets and towels).

Wealthier families might have a cupboard to hold the linens and display their pewter, glass, china, and silver. They might own a matching sofa and set of chairs upholstered in leather, wool, or needlework designed to look like Turkish carpets. Real imported carpets were draped over tables or beds. They were too valuable to waste on the floor.

Bed curtains, often red or green, kept out drafts and gave some privacy, for there was usually more than one bed in each room (including low trundle beds pushed under taller beds by day) and more than one sleeper in each. The master bed stood in the hall unless there were two downstairs rooms; then it graced the parlor. Walls were either covered with wood panels, or were plastered between the wooden supports. Sometimes the wood frame or the whole wall was tinted pale yellow, gray, green, cocoa brown, or red. The Reverend Parris had a map of the world on his wall in Salem Village, but farm families hung baskets, tools, and harnesses on their walls to get them out from underfoot.

Housewives cooked on little fires within the great hall hearth, unless they had a separate kitchen as there was in the Salem Village parsonage. People ate porridge for breakfast and supper, or had bread and cheese, or leftovers from the day before. They ate dinner, the main meal, at midday. On special occasions this

Cupboard owned by Putnam family. Chair owned by Philip and Mary English.

Iron cooking pot

could be a meat or fish pie. They usually dined on meat (chicken, pork, mutton, or beef, but rarely wild game) and vegetables (cabbages, onions, beans, or parsnips and the like). These all simmered together in the same pot with a pudding made of flour, fat, and sweetening that steamed in a cloth bag on top like a big dumpling. Fresh garden greens, called sauce, were available only in summer. By late winter, dried pea beans, either baked with pork or boiled to a mush, were sometimes the only available food. (Even into the 1700s, New England suffered spring famines off and on when food supplies ran out before the harvest.) Grains were sometimes made into boiled pudding. Most often grains were baked into bread, "the chief thing in a meal," according to the Reverend Parris, and "altogether necessary," whether "corn, barley, rye, [or] wheat." English rye and Indian corn together made the most common bread after a blight made wheat hard to grow and expensive to buy.

People ate with a knife, a spoon (or a crust of bread), and their fingers. Forks were still rare and "foreign." Richer people served meals on pewter or porcelain. Ordinary folk ate from pottery plates or wooden boards called trenchers (a step up from using the bread as a plate).

People often distrusted the cleanliness of water, especially in towns where wells might have been contaminated by outhouses. They preferred to drink apple or pear cider, beer of varying strengths, or imported wine if they could afford it. Milk was available mainly in the spring and summer, and most of it was made into butter or cheese.

Families usually ate in shifts, the master and mistress first, followed by their children and servants. In unusual households, like the Reverend Cotton Mather's in Boston, children joined their parents and even contributed to the conversation. In some backwoods homes, startled travelers noticed, everyone ate together, even the servants. The fact that people lived at the same time and in the same area did not mean that they lived in the same way.

German stoneware pot and New England pottery plate (drawings based on broken pieces found at Salem Village parsonage)

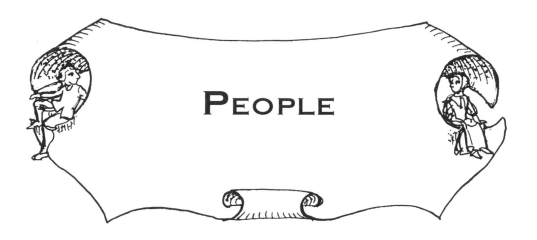

PEOPLE

Some historians have blamed the Salem trials on the Puritans' suspicions of anyone who was different. Yet there were more ethnic, economic, social, and religious differences among the people who lived in Massachusetts than are usually remembered.

Although Cotton Mather called his fellow settlers "American," most people still thought of themselves as English. But they, or their parents, had come from so many regions of Britain that their accents and customs seemed foreign to one other. The majority of people in Massachusetts Bay were from East Anglia in the southeast part of England, the source of town meetings, clapboards, and a nasal accent.

Some were Welsh, like the husband of witch-suspect Martha

Carrier. Some were Scottish servants who had been sent overseas after being taken prisoner during the English civil war. Only a few were Irish Catholic, like the servant Joan Sullivan, who thought Salem was a devilish place because no one said Mass in the meetinghouse.

Sailors visiting the port towns might come from as far away as Portugal, or even Ceylon. A few Dutch families lived in Boston, and John "the Greek" Amazeen (who may have been Italian) served as constable in Great Island, New Hampshire.

Caricature of man in European clothes made on stone by Algonquin, found in Lincoln, Massachusetts

The "French" were the largest non-English group, and included Protestant refugees from France or French Canada and French-speaking members of the Church of England from Jersey, an island off the coast of England. Although most changed their names—Philippe L'Anglais of Jersey became Philip English of Salem—they kept French as their first language.

John and Tituba Indian, the Reverend Parris's slaves, were "Spanish Indians" from the Spanish-ruled areas of South America and the Caribbean, not local Algonquin. Members of the Salem-area Naumkeag and Pawtuckett tribes were mentioned less and less in eastern Massachusetts records toward the end of the 1600s. Settlers already referred to the "last Indian" of various places, like Old Will of Will's Hill west of Salem Village (although his widow lived there well into the 1700s). The settlers feared the tribes from the north, whose fighting men were armed and supported by the French. And some native families that had been displaced from their planting grounds also took hostages to ransom for their own captured kin or for money to buy the supplies they could no longer grow.

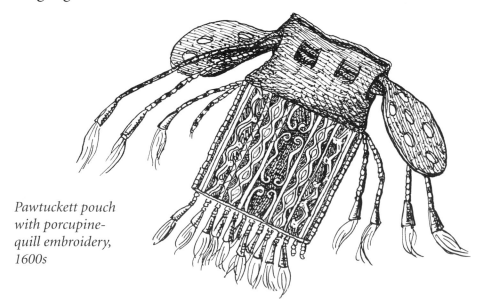

Pawtuckett pouch with porcupine-quill embroidery, 1600s

About two hundred black Africans and their descendants lived in Massachusetts by 1700, most as slaves, some free. "Jeremiah the Negro" was one of Boston's four licensed chimney sweeps in 1692. A very few free blacks owned land, had small businesses like chair making, and had earned enough money to help other Africans buy their freedom. A few became church members in Boston. But militia companies excluded blacks and Indians in 1656, and it was illegal for tavern keepers to serve alcohol to servants, apprentices, or nonwhites.

African-elephant ivory figure from the 1600s found in Pemaquid, Maine

As in Europe, whether people possessed money and worldly status divided them into the "better sort" addressed as Master (Mr.) and Mistress (Mrs.); the "middle sort" called Goodman and Goodwife (or Goody); and the "lower sort," including servants and the very poor, who were called by their given names like children.

The term "servants" covered a number of different situations: slaves, bond servants, apprentices, and hired help. Some, always nonwhite, were enslaved. A few of them bought or were given their freedom, but early attempts to outlaw slavery failed. White Europeans were "bond servants." They were required to serve a master for a certain number of years (usually seven) to pay for the expenses of immigration or some other debt. Young people learning a trade were apprentices who owed their masters the respect due an employer, teacher, and parent combined. Free hired help were employed by their masters and mistresses usually for a year at a time. (Reported deals with the Devil resembled servants' contracts.)

The status of the farmers, craftsmen, tradesmen, fishermen, and sailors fell between the rich and the slaves. Ministers and the most successful merchants counted as the "better sort," but class was less rigid than it was in England. New Englanders had an independent streak, and many people changed their status. Justice John Richards rose from an immigrant servant, to a merchant, to a judge of the witchcraft court. Society, like the economy, continued to change. Some people made fortunes, while others lost everything in the wars. Life was always uncertain.

LIFE CYCLE

In 1692, people's lives included danger—whatever country they lived in. In Massachusetts one child in ten died before he or she was a few days old, and a quarter or more of all children died before the legal age of twenty-one. These odds were better than for many parts of Europe or even other colonies, but death was a household fact. Infants might inherit a dead sibling's name along with the baby clothes.

All young children wore petticoats, including boys, until they were well out of diapers. Toddlers' clothes included "leading strings" (hanging from the shoulders) that an adult could grab to keep the child from falling into an open fire or down a well. No sooner were children old enough to walk and eat solid foods instead of their mothers' milk, than they had to accept a younger

sibling. By then they had also learned to say "No." Disobedience was punished, but the Mathers were among the few families who thought blows ought to be left for serious misbehavior.

Once they turned six or so, children could help with the constant labor of life. If fatherless or very poor, they became bond servants to a foster family in return for food, clothing, and education (as the Wardwell children were after their father was hanged for witchcraft).

Massachusetts required parents and masters to teach their children and servants to read. Towns of fifty or more families had to hire a schoolmaster to teach writing and arithmetic, but they were often underpaid and did not stay. Children usually learned to read from their mothers or from a neighbor woman who kept a dame school at home. "Dame" was the polite term for a woman teacher, who earned a tenth or less of a schoolmaster's pay.

Students learned reading and then writing, so many people could read who could not write. More people could read and write in New England than in England or in Europe. As part of his plan to rise in the world, William Phips (who became governor) learned to read and write at age twenty-one. Cotton Mather sent all his children to school and taught his daughters Latin, Greek, and Hebrew, but this was unusual. Philip English sent his daughters to a Boston boarding school specializing in fancy needlework and other cultured female skills. Few could afford such schooling.

Larger towns had a grammar school where boys learned Latin, especially those boys intended for Harvard College in Cambridge, Massachusetts—the only college then in British North America. Its founders had feared later generations would, without realizing it, become cut off from European thought. About half the graduates became merchants or farmers. The rest became ministers, as was the school's main purpose. Still, Cambridge was often plagued with noisy student parties.

Harvard College

Graduating college classes were small: only six men received a degree in 1692. Instead, most young men trained as apprentices to farmers or craftsmen. At sixteen, all boys who were not in college had to join the militia, and all young men and women were punished as adults were if they broke the law. They still had to answer to their parents or guardians until they were twenty-one, however.

Parents could not force two young people to marry, but they could forbid a match if they did not approve of it. Puritan couples were usually married in civil ceremonies performed by a magistrate, not a minister; since the marriage concerned only their life on earth, not in heaven. Puritan ministers were allowed to perform the ceremony only after 1686, due to Anglican influence. The accompanying celebrations ranged from quiet cheer between the families over cakes and ale to rowdy neighborhood noise-making.

Puritans counted sex among God's good creations, but expected it to occur within marriage, which it usually did. In an ideal marriage, the partners were genuinely concerned with one another's comfort and well-being. Still, the husband was head of the family. Unlike British law, Massachusetts' original laws made it illegal for husbands to hit their wives—except in self-defense—and required that husbands leave their widows enough to live on.

Widows could sell their own property, but needed the legislature's approval as would a child, an "idiot," or a "distracted person." Widows with property paid taxes, but no woman could vote anywhere in European-based culture. Women would have even fewer rights during the next two centuries. They made their opinions felt behind the scenes, however, in ways that seldom reached the written records. In Chebago, Massachusetts, women began to build a meetinghouse when the townsmen were under a court order not to.

To provide for their families, grown men worked for as many hours as there was daylight. They attended town meetings, served in the military, and helped with community chores like road mending and barn raising. Some added the tasks of public office, which was always part time whether the position was selectman or governor. Men dealt with the outside world and were their household's public voice.

Although some women ran shops, wove, worked as healers, or even defended absent husbands in court, they worked mostly at the constant tasks of the home. With the help of daughters and hired girls, they kept their households clothed and fed. On farms, they also produced most of the food in the dairy and the kitchen garden.

In addition, wives usually gave birth every two years, tended by a midwife and surrounded by other women to help and encourage them. Even so, one woman in five died during childbirth. The culture expected a couple to have many children because so many babies died, and because older children helped on the farm. But parents' attachment to their children was not just practical. Some mothers were haunted by visions of their dead children, and parents who thought their children were bewitched could be fiercely protective.

The average life span (not counting infants who died) was about seventy years for men, and sixty-three for women—far better than in Europe and in other New World colonies. As a result, New England had more families with several generations than did other places. But a single parent with young children had trouble keeping a household together, even with hired help.

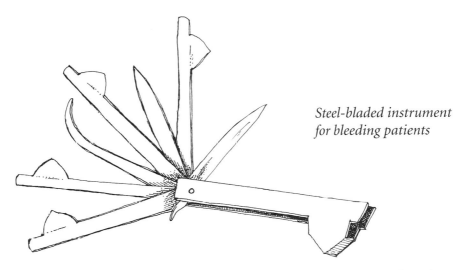

Steel-bladed instrument for bleeding patients

Many of the widows and widowers remarried, and stepfamilies were common.

To fight the diseases that might strike any age, people used home cures, folk healers, and trained doctors. Folk healers included women who specialized in midwifery but also were paid to treat injuries and illnesses. Other folk healers, like Roger Toothaker, dealt with countermagic and witch finding as well. The physicians who discovered what was troubling patients, the surgeons who operated on them (usually by bleeding them of "excess" blood or by setting broken limbs), and the apothecaries who prepared and sold the mostly herbal medicines, all learned their trades from books as well as from apprenticeships. Few had an academic title, but all were called doctor as a courtesy. One or two, like Phillip Reed of Lynn, accused their female competitors of witchcraft. But Cotton Mather, who studied medicine before becoming a minister, had only praise for the herbal skills of

Mrs. Anne Eliot and thought being an apothecary a good trade for his own daughter.

Medicine, like the other sciences, was changing. Cotton Mather believed that illness might be caused by the tiny creatures he saw through his microscope. But no one paid attention to that idea, or made a connection between infections and the habit of letting young children relieve themselves in the garden. Indoor plumbing did not exist. Sanitation was a back-yard outhouse and chamber pots. Bathtubs were unknown, but the cleaner folk washed from a basin.

If the symptoms were unusual enough, and if there were already rumors about a particular suspect, the medical expert— doctor or folk healer, man or woman—might decide that the patient was bewitched. But a diagnosis of magic was unusual. People were injured by farm tools, Indian raids, and frostbite. They drowned, died in childbirth, were struck by lightning, or froze to death in blizzards. They were weakened by intestinal

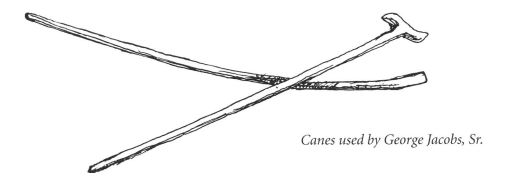

Canes used by George Jacobs, Sr.

parasites or tortured by gallstones. They died slowly of tuberculosis or cancer, or quickly in outbreaks of diphtheria, measles, or smallpox.

Still, some people lived surprisingly long lives. The Reverend Wigglesworth never had a well day, but served Medford as minister and physician for half a century. Although over eighty, old George Jacobs was still bossing his family around when he was arrested for witchcraft in 1692.

When people did die, their bodies were prepared at home. The tasks of death, like birth, fell mostly to women. Towns set aside

Slate tombstone for Mrs. Elizabeth Parris, wife of the Reverend Samuel Parris of Salem Village, in the Wadsworth Cemetery, Danvers

public land as burying grounds. By 1692, Boston had three and Salem two, although in rural areas like Salem Village, people buried their dead in private family plots.

The body, washed and wrapped in a shroud, was sealed in a six-sided coffin. Six bearers carried it to the grave while the bell—if the community had one—rang slowly. Later, there might be a sermon in honor of the dead, but little was said at the actual burial. The minister, family, and friends stood around the grave while the earth was put back in it, then they gathered at the dead person's home for cake and punch. Later the family set a carved wooden or stone marker on the grave.

Richer families gave the principal guests and coffin bearers a gift of a scarf, a pair of gloves, or a ring decorated with skulls. Even the poor served refreshments. When witch-suspect Sarah Good buried her first husband, she spent more on rum than on the grave.

After death, people believed, souls went off to a heavenly judgment, to face the spiritual results of the earthly life just ended.

Gold funeral ring made by John Coney of Boston in 1694

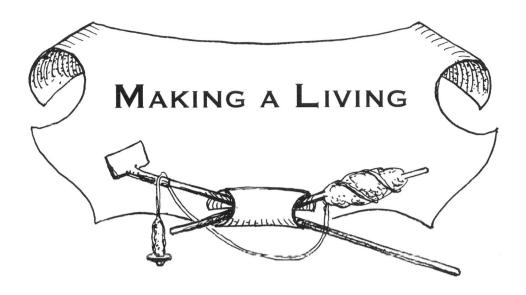

MAKING A LIVING

Long or short, people's lives were filled with work: work accomplished by the pull of horse or ox, by the push of wind or water, by the strength and skill of the worker's own hands. Most people farmed, but even the most successful farmers could not make everything they needed. They had to buy the barrels, horseshoes, and other gear made by craftsmen who lived in the towns. The craftsmen bought the food the farmers grew, and both wanted the goods that merchants imported.

To learn their crafts, boys were apprenticed in their early teens. Girls learned to be housewives at home or they were sometimes apprenticed to learn it in another household. Besides learning child minding and open-hearth cookery, mending clothes and boiling laundry, country girls had to know how to keep a vegetable garden, hen house, and dairy; how to preserve meat, fruits, and vegetables; and how to brew beer and cider.

Single women, including many of the women who were supposed to be "bewitched," worked mostly as live-in help. They received a small salary plus room and board and the tips their master's visitors gave them. Some households included maids as part of the family, but a few mistreated them. A few servants, like-wise, stole from their employers and terrorized the children.

Besides their household jobs, some married women spun linen, cotton, or wool thread; taught a dame school; doctored their neighbors; ran their husband's tavern; washed other people's laundry; or kept a shop. Although these jobs earned only about 60 percent of what men's work did, they became even more impor-tant if a husband died. Widow Mary Gedney of Salem, who sold refreshments to the witchcraft court in 1692, sold liquor to support her three young children.

British import laws stated that all foreign goods had to enter

Massachusetts at either Boston or Salem. Although the laws were often ignored, most merchants worked in those towns, especially Boston. In the 1690s, Boston also had nineteen booksellers and more kinds of craftsmen than anywhere else in Massachusetts. The merchants imported writing paper and silks, books and toys, chocolate and fine wines, sugar and molasses, bond servants or slaves. Bound for the Caribbean islands, their ships held Rhode Island riding horses or Maine lumber. Or they carried meat and fish preserved in salt to feed the island slaves who grew the sugar and processed it into molasses. Sometimes ships carried rum distilled from that molasses to Africa. There, slavers used it to barter for captured Africans whom they sold as slaves to Caribbean islands and elsewhere.

Foreign voyages might last for months. Coastal traders and fishermen made shorter trips, but all sailors risked capture by pirates or by French privateers—men licensed by their government to attack foreign shipping. (Some New England ship owners

were themselves privateers who seized French ships.) The sea created much of New England's work: for the wharf hands, shoremen, sailors, and fishermen who lived along the coast; for the shipwrights who built the vessels; for the rope makers and sail makers who equipped them; and the brewers, bakers, and salt-meat makers who stocked the ships with food for their voyages.

Salem was smaller than Boston, but had its own ship-building

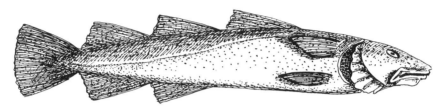

Wooden codfish, which honored a fish important to the Massachusetts economy in the 1600s and 1700s

industry. All the leather crafts existed in Salem as well, so locals could buy shoes and saddles without going to Boston. Salem gunsmiths made and repaired muskets, goldsmiths made tankards as well as rings (but usually of silver), and blacksmiths made everything from iron horseshoes to anchors. There were carpenters to build a house; cabinet makers to furnish it; and an upholsterer to pad the chairs. This last was George Herrick, who was also marshal and deputy sheriff in 1692. Bakers and brewers kept shops too, for not all houses had bake ovens and not all housewives brewed beer. Mrs. Mary English (Philip's wife) ran a shop built into a corner of her fine new mansion and sold a variety of goods, from ready-made shoes to thimbles.

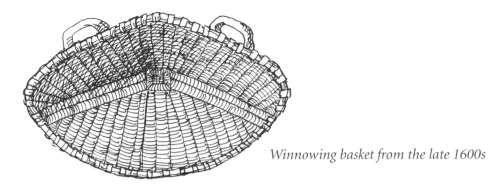

Winnowing basket from the late 1600s

Most country folk farmed. They had apple and pear orchards, milk cattle, grain fields, kitchen gardens for their own vegetables and herbs, and beehives. In Salem Village, Thomas Putnam owned a flock of sheep. A few craftsmen also had shops in Salem Village: a cooper (who made barrels), a potter, a carpenter, a sawyer (who cut boards), a physician, a shoemaker, and a weaver. Farmers often practiced a second trade, especially in the slow seasons. Every shilling helped, even if it was in barter.

New Englanders were short on currency. Most of their coins were English. Twelve copper pence (pennies), for example, equaled one silver shilling. Twenty shillings made one pound. (A

workman might earn two shillings a day.) Massachusetts illegally minted "pine-tree shillings" for a while and people also used foreign coins, like Spanish pieces of eight. To pay debts from the ongoing frontier war with Canada, Massachusetts printed paper money in 1690—the first in the country. But few trusted it and the bills' value fell rapidly.

Although bartering lasted into the 1800s, New England's economy continued to change. While a few merchants became wealthy, more and more farmers found the acres available to them too cramped to prosper. During the war with Canada, fishing and shipping suffered from privateer attacks. French and Indian forces burned whole towns in Maine and New Hampshire.

Evil spirits, said the bewitched, not only threatened their souls in that risky, uncertain time, but tried to bribe them with coins and finery.

RECREATION

People did, however, relax from their work. Cotton Mather's great delight was reading—scientific as well as religious books. But no one thought it was odd if the Reverend Peter Thatcher of Milton bowled at ninepins in his garden. People agreed that a reasonable amount of exercise (for men at least) restored the mind and spirit. The Reverend John Wise had been so skilled a wrestler in his student days, that some challenged him even after he became minister of Chebago.

Teams of young men kicked large, soft footballs, and individual youths danced jigs in informal contests. "Mixed dancing" (of both sexes) was discouraged as too "suggestive," but dancing itself, according to the Reverend Increase Mather, was as natural and acceptable an expression of joy as laughter.

Instrumental music seemed unfit for religious services, but elsewhere ministers, merchants, sailors, and craftsmen enjoyed a variety of imported instruments, from viols and fiddles to dulcimers and lutes. The Reverend Charles Morton of Charlestown had two bass viols, three violins, a harpsichord, and a large collection of sheet music.

Those who could afford to had their portraits painted, in oils or watercolors, life-sized or miniature. Women used their needles to embroider decoratively as well as to darn. They invented their own patterns or bought printed kits with the colored wools included.

Part of a sampler embroidered about 1644 by fourteen-year-old Mary Hollingsworth, who was accused of witchcraft in 1692

Some people used tobacco, either chewed a wad of it (and spat), sniffed its dust as snuff, or smoked it in a pipe. Suspected "witch" Sarah Good smoked a pipe, as had Mary Rowlandson, wife of Lancaster's minister. Some ministers smoked, but Cotton Mather thought the habit was a dirty one and distrusted its long-term effects, although some physicians claimed it dried up colds.

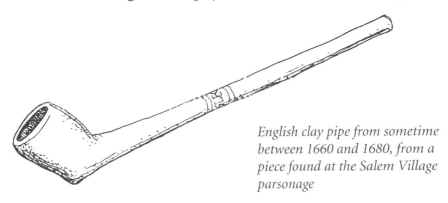

English clay pipe from sometime between 1660 and 1680, from a piece found at the Salem Village parsonage

Wasting time was always discouraged. So was any kind of gambling, or anything that could interrupt the Sabbath (Sunday). People entertained each other daily with conversation—or gossip—while they worked. They visited each other in the evenings and during the slow winter season, celebrated an occasional wedding, and had time to chat in the break between Sabbath sermons.

Their modest pleasures were not an escape from routine, but instead fit within it.

THE ROUND OF TIME

S abbath religious services were the high point of most people's week, and all nonemergency work was expected to stop from Saturday evening to Sunday evening. Many took off another half day to attend the Thursday afternoon lecture, a custom begun in England when Puritan ministers were forbidden to deliver Sunday sermons. Ministers took turns giving these lectures within their areas, and enough people traveled to hear different ministers (and refresh themselves at local taverns afterward) that the government once tried to limit the number of lectures as disruptive to work.

Bigger towns, like Salem, held a weekly market where country folk sold food to townspeople and bought town-made goods. Larger fairs that included animals were scheduled four times a year when the county court met to hear local cases. Also, all able-bodied white men between sixteen and sixty—except for ministers and college students—were called up for military practice (called musters) about every six weeks. Although men were sometimes selected for frontier service at these times, the musters were also an opportunity for boys to show off to watching girls during the drills or during the wrestling, football, or sharpshooting afterward.

Besides the weekly Sabbath services, the religious year included the monthly taking of communion by church members after the regular service. Churches sometimes held days of thanksgiving or fasting to offer thanks or apologies to God for specific events. (Thanksgiving was not a set annual holiday until 1932.) Now and then the legislature declared a lecture day as a general thanksgiving or fast day throughout Massachusetts for events of wider importance like worry over the beginning of the witchcraft trials in 1692, and an apology for them in 1697.

What Puritans did not celebrate were the civil holidays (such as the king's birthday) and religious holy days of old England. Michaelmas (September 29) was, however, the traditional end of

The Reverend Cotton Mather's silver pocket

summer, and it was an old custom for business agreements to extend from one Candlemas (February 2) to another. Puritans found nothing in the Bible that told them to celebrate Christmas, so they kept their shops open on December 25. Anglicans and Huguenots did hold Christmas services.

All of these observances fit into the greater cycle of the natural world, in the country as well as in the towns.

January

Woodcutters and their oxen sledded logs from snowy wood lots, but farmers often worked close to home during the short, cold days. They split shingles and sawed planks for future use. They threshed dried white peas, wheat, and barley on the barn's threshing floor, swinging the jointed flail down to strike the seeds from the dried stalks. Farmers stood in the great open doors and tossed last summer's grain in flat winnowing baskets to let the sharp breeze snatch away the light useless chaff. As farmers branded their year-old animals, farmyards filled with pained bawling and the reek of singed hair and flesh.

This was often a time for fortune telling, a custom the ministers discouraged, though some parishioners tried it anyway.

February

Farmers finished threshing oats and peas, and began to separate the broken fibers of flax and hemp. Those with wood lots and access to water got ready to float extra logs downstream to town markets, and those with extra hay sold it to those who had run short. Any extra time was used to check fences and property lines, a task that could either end or begin arguments.

Towns held their main town meeting in late winter, after the deepest snows had melted and before planting season started.

March

Farm animals began to give birth. Careful farmers finished their repairs and put the plowing gear in order. They broke up the fields' hard earth and burned the old corn hills, while housewives turned over the smaller kitchen gardens. Whoever had fishing rights to an alewife stream harvested the small, migratory fish and preserved them in salt. Spring rain and melted snow filled the loud streams and turned the roads to mud. But Essex County folk still took their livestock and other goods to the market in Ipswich when the county court met on the month's last Tuesday.

April

As migrating birds returned, farmers plowed the fields below; spread dung and other waste to fertilize them; and sowed peas, barley, flax, and hemp. Farm children drove the cattle to graze on newly green pastures. March and April were the farmers' busiest months. As they planted row after row of corn, the song of the brown thrasher seemed a mockery: "Drop it, drop it. Cover it up, cover it up. Pull it up, pull it up, pull it up."

May

Farm wives made butter and cheese now that the cows were again giving milk—sweet and rich from the new upland grass the cows ate, without the winter tang from salt-marsh hay. Farmers threshed the last of the winter wheat as summer wheat sprouted—along with weeds that could crowd out wheat and corn alike if not hoed down. Farmers sheared their sheep before the hot weather, snipping the fleece at its base to remove it in one piece like a coat.

Early in the month, Election Day for province-level offices was held in Boston. Many people enjoyed the excuse to visit—wives included, even though they could not vote.

June

The first fresh peas of the season were ready to eat from the garden, along with strawberries and blueberries from the wild.

Whole families, even ministers, might spend a day berrying. Farmers hauled timber and repaired stone walls with the everlasting rocky crop that came out of the soil like mushrooms. It was time to wean the spring calves from their mothers and to buy and sell new livestock. Salem held a market for this on the month's last Tuesday, when court sat. Farmers eyed the ripening corn, sowed turnips, and planted cabbages for the next winter's supplies.

It was always time to weed.

July

Farmers rose at dawn to swelter through blistering days and, if necessary, into the nights to mow and stack their hay under the full moon. They scythed the grass in practiced sweeps, followed by everyone who could be spared to rake it. Rain could rot it all, or lightning strike the haymakers.

Seed time and harvest overlapped as farmers sowed turnips and reaped wheat, rye, and oats. They cut the white peas (vine and all) to thresh later. They harvested the summer hemp used for rope and the flax that made linen, then soaked the long stalks in shallow ponds to separate their fibers.

Hundreds crowded Cambridge for Harvard's commencement: the graduating students' families, magistrates, alumni, local merrymakers, and peddlers enjoyed the sermons, speeches, Latin debates, and dinners—especially the plum cake and wine.

August

Farmers mowed a second harvest of hay. They brought in wheat and more peas, and began to pick apples. They rounded up the horses left running half-wild in the woods, sold some of the cattle, and bought the salt they would need to preserve meat for the winter. Men hunted passenger pigeons with guns, nets, clubs, and captive decoys to kill dozens at a time.

September

Women on farms began cider making. They crushed the fruit to separate the juice and pulp, then stored the liquid while it "worked" (created alcohol). Except for root crops like turnips, most food would not keep over the winter unless it was dried, salted, pickled, or fermented.

The men brought in the last of the hay and sowed next year's winter wheat. Farmers who lived along the coast and owned salt marshes sowed salt-marsh hay. They clumped Indian-corn stalks in ghostly, rustling shocks on the bare fields.

The county court for Essex met in Newbury on the last Tuesday of the month.

October

It was ripening season for wild bayberries, a source of energy for migrating birds, or of sweet-scented candles for the housewife who wanted something cheaper than beeswax but better than animal fat. Some housewives brewed a winter's supply of strong beer to store away, but others simply brewed milder "small beer" every week or so. Farmers pulled turnips and picked squash and apples. They carted corn to the barn to await husking. Neighbors often shared the work, and husking bees tended to be loud and jolly occasions.

November

Women with a supply of wool or flax would spin a winter's worth of yarn or thread even if they had to hire other women to help. Outdoors, men repaired walls, hedges, and bridges before winter set in, carried manure from the yards to the dung hill, sowed winter hemp, and pulled parsnips, which were always sweeter after a frost.

November was a month of death. Hunters stalked deer, and every farmyard was a scene of slaughter. Carcasses of cattle, sheep, and pigs were hung by their heels from chains, so the blood could drain from their slit throats. The whole family was involved as the carcasses were gutted and skinned, and the meat was cut up and salted or made into sausage. Horns, hides, and hog bristles all had their uses. Even the blood was used in meat puddings.

December

Farmers began to thresh the wheat, rye, and oats, and to break the hemp stalks soaked the summer before. They settled the surviving livestock in barns for the winter and brought them hay from stacks carefully arranged to shed rain and snow. Farm wives salted down the remaining pork and beef in kegs and kept an eye on the fermenting cider in the cellar as it hissed and "sang."

If all were well, the barn was in good repair and the house was supplied with enough firewood. The Essex County court met in Salem at the end of the month, but winter was usually less hurried than summer. People had more time to visit their neighbors, if it didn't storm. Blizzards could keep people housebound, unable to reach even Sabbath meetings.

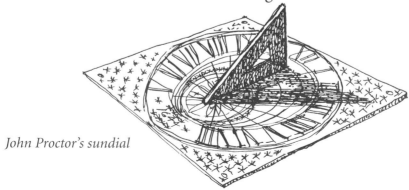

John Proctor's sundial

GOVERNMENT

While the seasons of a new land changed what had been the people's everyday British customs, New England's great distance from Britain encouraged new ideas of government.

The 1692 witchcraft cases are often blamed on a Puritan-controlled government because church membership was the basic requirement for voting or serving on juries (instead of rank and wealth as elsewhere). But by the standards of the time, church and state were separate in Massachusetts. Ministers were not part of the government. They were never elected to public office, except for a few who left the pulpit for public life. Government officials, although they were church members, felt free to ignore the ministers' advice.

The government of Massachusetts, in fact, continued to change. Originally the government was supposed to protect the Congregational churches' right to exist. Church attendance was required in the early generations, but membership never was. The government had often treated public expressions of different religious views as threats to public peace, but by 1692 all Protestant churches were allowed. (Anglican Virginia, on the other hand, simply expelled all Nonconformists, Quakers included.)

In Salem, as in other towns, all free men over the legal age of twenty-one gathered to vote on town matters and for town officers. (Women were not a part of these meetings, but sometimes underage, nonwhite, or other ineligible males joined a voice vote in the heat of the moment.) They elected a board of men called selectmen to handle local business, constables to keep order and collect local taxes, and a variety of minor officials (like hog reeve to round up stray pigs).

Boston's first town house, where the General Court also met

Towns each sent two representatives to the legislature's spring and fall sessions in Boston unless they hired a Boston man to represent them. Representatives also served as local magistrates—like the officials who first questioned the witch suspects. The representatives, along with a smaller council, made up the "General Court"—the legislature. By 1692, England insisted on appointing the governor.

What changed most over time were the rules for who could vote for or hold offices above town level, and who could be a juror. For a long time, men needed to be church members, but in 1692 voters and jurors were either church members *or* they owned a certain amount of property. Toward the end of the trials, after the laws were revised, all a man needed was property.

Even so, about the same number of people voted as before, and the same men continued to be elected.

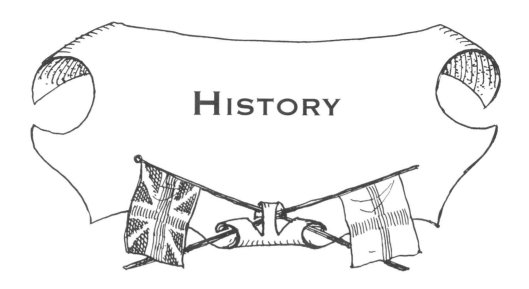

HISTORY

Many truly troubling situations added to the strains of the times. For one thing, people did not know what to expect from the British government. From 1686 to 1689, England had combined all its colonies north of Pennsylvania into one colony—the Dominion of New England—and sent Sir Edmund Andros to govern it. During his rule, the General Court was not allowed to meet, and no one was allowed to vote. Farmers and homeowners were told that they no longer owned their land, but could pay rent for it to the government. Gossips, even among Andros's own men, guessed that everyone would be ordered to become Anglican. In England, only Anglicans could hold most offices, teach, attend the universities, or legally marry.

News of a revolution in England was followed by resistance in America. Boston revolted on April 18, 1689, and forced Governor Andros to surrender. Massachusetts temporarily restored its General Court, shipped Andros and his men back to England, and waited to see what would happen next.

For a long time, France had claimed part of Maine and wanted the rest of British North America. French Canada sent small raiding parties of French-Canadian woodsmen and their Abenaki allies to attack villages in Maine, New York, and New Hampshire. (York, in southern Maine, was burned and many of its people taken hostage in January 1692—around the time the girls in Salem Village first began acting bewitched.) The French king, moreover, had outlawed all Protestant churches in his lands. The bewitched and the confessing "witches" would often describe

Seal used by Governor Andros showing King James II with his New England subjects, who, in fact, did not behave so obediently

seeing devils that looked and acted like the raiding parties.

Most attempts by the English colonies to retaliate were less successful. On the eve of the witchcraft scare, the ongoing war drained the Massachusetts treasury. French privateer attacks on local shipping were ruining the fishing industry. Refugees from Maine and New Hampshire flocked to Boston and Salem.

Increase Mather represented Massachusetts in London to negotiate a new charter, which would give Massachusetts the right to exist and to govern itself. He was able to keep some of the legislature's powers, and to avoid having all of English North America ruled by a London-based committee. King William insisted that any governor be a military man of his own choosing, but allowed Mather to recommend the first. Mather suggested Sir William Phips, a self-made New Englander who had been knighted as a reward for the sunken treasure he had salvaged in the Caribbean.

Governor Phips and Increase Mather returned to Boston with the new charter in June of 1692 and found the treasury all but empty, the frontier still threatened, and the jails of three counties full of witch suspects.

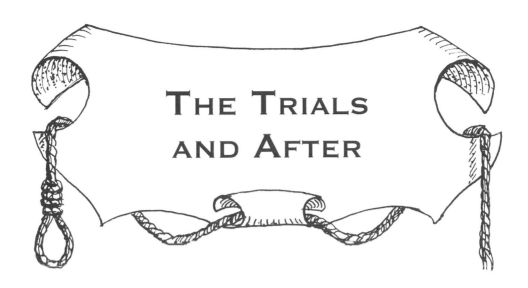

The Trials
and After

The Salem witchcraft panic began with personal fear, grew with neighborhood suspicion, and then spread through the region fueled by the time's tensions.

The idea of a witch conspiracy was always unusual, but a possible attack from Hell seemed less surprising when the people's religion, economy, and even their lives were at risk from so many earthly threats. Salem Villagers, in addition, were quarreling with other towns about boundaries, with Salem over local rule, and with each other about what pay had been promised to the minister.

Throughout the spring and summer of 1692, about 60 people appeared to be bewitched. Not all of them testified in court, but 6 "bewitched" people actually died. About 150 of more than 200 witch suspects were arrested. Most lived in Salem Village and other parts of Salem, nearly as many in Andover, and the rest were scattered throughout three counties. (About 10 other people were accused in western Connecticut, far from Salem.)

Suspects ranged from wealthy to impoverished, from saintly to cantankerous. Most were older women. Two of the executed men were apparently wife-beaters. Some suspects were noticeably eccentric, but so were some of the bewitched. A few "witches" practiced folk magic, but so did some of the accusers. Some were never arrested at all, and one man taken in for questioning was released. Many "confessed," while others died rather than lie. It was all a tangle of confusion.

But even such a "hidden work of darkness" as the 1692 trials, people felt, had to have some lesson in it at least. Eventually even those who had most trusted spectral evidence realized how contradictory it was. They slowly understood that panic must not

Sarah
Good

Susanna
Martin

Sarah
Wildes

John
Proctor

George
Jacobs, Sr.

Bridget
Bishop

Rebecca
Nurse

Elizabeth
Howe

Rev. George
Burroughs

John
Willard

be allowed to let fear and resentment judge unproven acts. Their real pain and fear did not mean their accusations were true. Twenty people had been killed and others died of disease in jail because this had been forgotten.

But disasters caused by even good intentions still required an apology (the sooner the better), and some kind of payment to patch up damaged lives. Together, the Public Fast in 1697, the Reversal of Attainder in 1711, and the restitution payments of 1712 were only the third official apology in the history of western witchcraft trials. Nevertheless, the Salem cases became a symbol for all witchcraft trials even when other, larger scares were forgotten.

Understanding the events in the context of their times, and realizing that the people involved were not just cardboard heroes and villains, is a reminder that all such tragedies begin with ordinary people—like us.

Giles Corey   Mary Easty   Ann Pudeator   Wilmot Read   Mary Parker

Martha Carrier   Martha Corey   Alice Parker   Margaret Scott   Samuel Wardwell

·Selected Sources·

Reconstructing the past depends on surviving evidence, either written (like public papers and personal diaries) or material (like museum objects and archaeological finds), and the conclusions of experts who study such clues. Of the more than sixty works used for this book, all fairly technical, the following were among the most helpful.

Most of the court papers for the 1692 trials are collected in Paul Boyer and Stephen Nissenbaum, eds., *The Salem Witchcraft Papers*, 3 vols. (New York: Da Capo Press, 1977).

George Lincoln Burr, ed., *Narratives of the Witchcraft Trials* (New York: Charles Scribner's Sons, 1914), includes selections from several contemporary accounts such as Cotton Mather's *Wonders of the Invisible World*, Robert Calef's *More Wonders of the Invisible World*, John Hale's *A Modest Enquiry*, and Deodat Lawson's *A Brief and True Narrative*.

Two useful collections are Perry Miller and Thomas H. Johnson, eds., *The Puritans*, 2 vols. (New York: Harper & Row, 1963), selections by seventeenth-century New England writers; and Alden T. Vaughan and Francis J. Bremer, eds., *Puritan New England* (New York: St. Martin's Press, 1977), twentieth-century writings on seventeenth-century life.

Some of the better modern studies of the Salem trials are: Paul Boyer and Stephen Nissenbaum, *Salem Possessed* (Cambridge, Mass.: Harvard University Press, 1974); John Putnam Demos, *Entertaining Satan* (New York: Oxford University Press, 1982); Chadwick Hansen, *Witchcraft at Salem* (New York: George Braziller, 1969); Carol F. Karlsen, *The Devil in the Shape of a Woman* (New York: W. W. Norton, 1987); Richard Weisman, *Witchcraft, Magic, and Religion in 17th Century Massachusetts* (Amherst, Mass.: University of Massachusetts Press, 1984).

For the religion of the era see: Philip F. Gura, *A Glimpse of Sion's Glory* (Middletown, Conn.: Wesleyan University Press, 1984); David D. Hall, *Faithful Shepherd* (New York: W. W. Norton, 1972) and *Worlds of Wonder, Days of Judgment* (New York: Alfred A. Knopf, 1989); Edmund S. Morgan, *Visible Saints* (Ithaca, N.Y.: Cornell University Press, 1963).

Diaries give a good feel for the times, especially Joseph Green, "Diary of Joseph Green of Salem Village," Essex Institute, *Historical Collections*, vol. 8 (1866), pp. 215-224; vol. 10 (1869), pp. 79–109; vol. 31 (1900), pp. 323–330. See also Cotton Mather, *Dairy of Cotton Mather*, 2 vols., ed. W. C. Ford, Massachusetts Historical Society, *Collections*, 7th series, vol. 7 (1911) and vol. 8 (1912); Samuel Sewall, *Diary of Samuel Sewall*, 2 vols., ed. Halsey Thomas (New York: Farrar, Straus & Giroux, 1973).

Everyday life was wonderfully presented by the Boston Museum of Fine Arts's exhibit and 3-volume catalog *New England Begins*, Jonathan Fairbanks and Robert F. Treat (Boston: Museum of Fine Arts, 1982). See also Abbott Lowell Cummings, *The Frame Houses of Massachusetts Bay* (Cambridge, Mass.: Harvard University Press, 1979); John Demos, *A Little Commonwealth* (New York: Oxford University Press, 1970); David Hackett Fischer, *Albion's Seed* (New York: Oxford University Press, 1988); Richard B. Trask, *The Devil Amongst Us: A History of the Salem Village Parsonage* (Danvers, Mass.: Danvers Historical Society, 1971); and Laurel Thatcher Ulrich, *Good Wives* (New York: Alfred A. Knopf, 1982). For the Salem area see Sidney Perley, *The History of Salem, Massachusetts*, 3 vols. (Haverhill, Mass.: Record Publishing, 1928), and his articles in *Essex Antiquarian*, vol. 2 (1898) to vol. 12 (1908), and in Essex Institute, *Historical Collections*, vol. 49 (1913) to vol. 56 (1920).

For law see Edwin Powers, *Crime and Punishment in Early Massachusetts* (Boston: Beacon Press, 1966). For business see Barnard Bailyn, *New England Merchants in the Seventeenth Century* (Cambridge, Mass.: Harvard University Press, 1955).

New England history is covered in W. H. Whitmore, ed.,

Andros Tracts, 3 vols. (Boston: Prince Society, 1868); Thomas Hutchinson, *The History of the Colony and Province of Massachusetts-Bay*, 3 vols., ed. Lawrence Shaw Mayo (Cambridge, Mass.: Harvard University Press, 1936).

For allowing me to quote from manuscripts in their collections, I wish to thank the Connecticut Historical Society, Hartford, Connecticut, for Samuel Parris, "Sermons, 1689-1695," pp. 149, 248, 184; and to thank the Massachusetts State Archives, Dorchester, Massachusetts, for Major Robert Pike's December 19, 1690, account of cleaning Boston's jail, in Massachusetts Archives, vol. 36, p. 254.

Cotton Mather's seal that was attached to his watch

· INDEX·